my first
word
book

Angela Wilkes

DK

DORLING KINDERSLEY, INC.
NEW YORK

A DORLING KINDERSLEY BOOK

Art Editor Penny Britchfield
Editor Sheila Hanly
Art Director Roger Priddy
Managing Editor Jane Yorke
Production Controller Marguerite Fenn
Additional Design David Gillingwater, Mandy Earey

Photography Dave King, Tim Ridley, Jo Foord,
Steve Gorton, Paul Bricknell
Additional Photography Philip Dowell, Michael Dunning,
Stephen Oliver, Steve Shott, Jerry Young
Illustrations Pat Thorne

First American Edition, 1991
10 9
Dorling Kindersley Inc., 232 Madison Avenue
New York, New York 10016

ISBN: 1-879431-21-1
ISBN: 1-879431-36-X (lib. bdg.)
Library of Congress Catalog Card Number: 91-60897

Dorling Kindersley would like to thank Helen Drew,
Kim Marshall, and Brian Griver for their help in producing this book,
and Leah Bellamy, Carmen Berzon, Laura Douglas, Charlotte Harris,
Holly Jackman, Andrew Linnet, Paul Miller, Robert Nagle, Hiral Patel,
Sam Priddy, Kayleigh Swan, George and Elizabeth Wilkes,
and Kimberley Yarde for appearing in this book.

Contents

All about me	4
My clothes	6
At home	8
Around the house	10
In the kitchen	12
Things to eat and drink	14
In the bathroom	16
In the garden	18
In the toolshed	20
Going out	22

At the park	24		At the seaside	46
At the supermarket	26		Time, weather, and seasons	48
Cars	28		Sports	50
Things that move	30		Actions	52
In the country	32		Playtime	54
In the woods	34		Storytime	55
On the farm	36		Colors, shapes, and numbers	56
Pets	38		Positions	58
At the zoo	40		Opposites	60
My toys	42		Index	62
Going to school	44			

All about me

My face

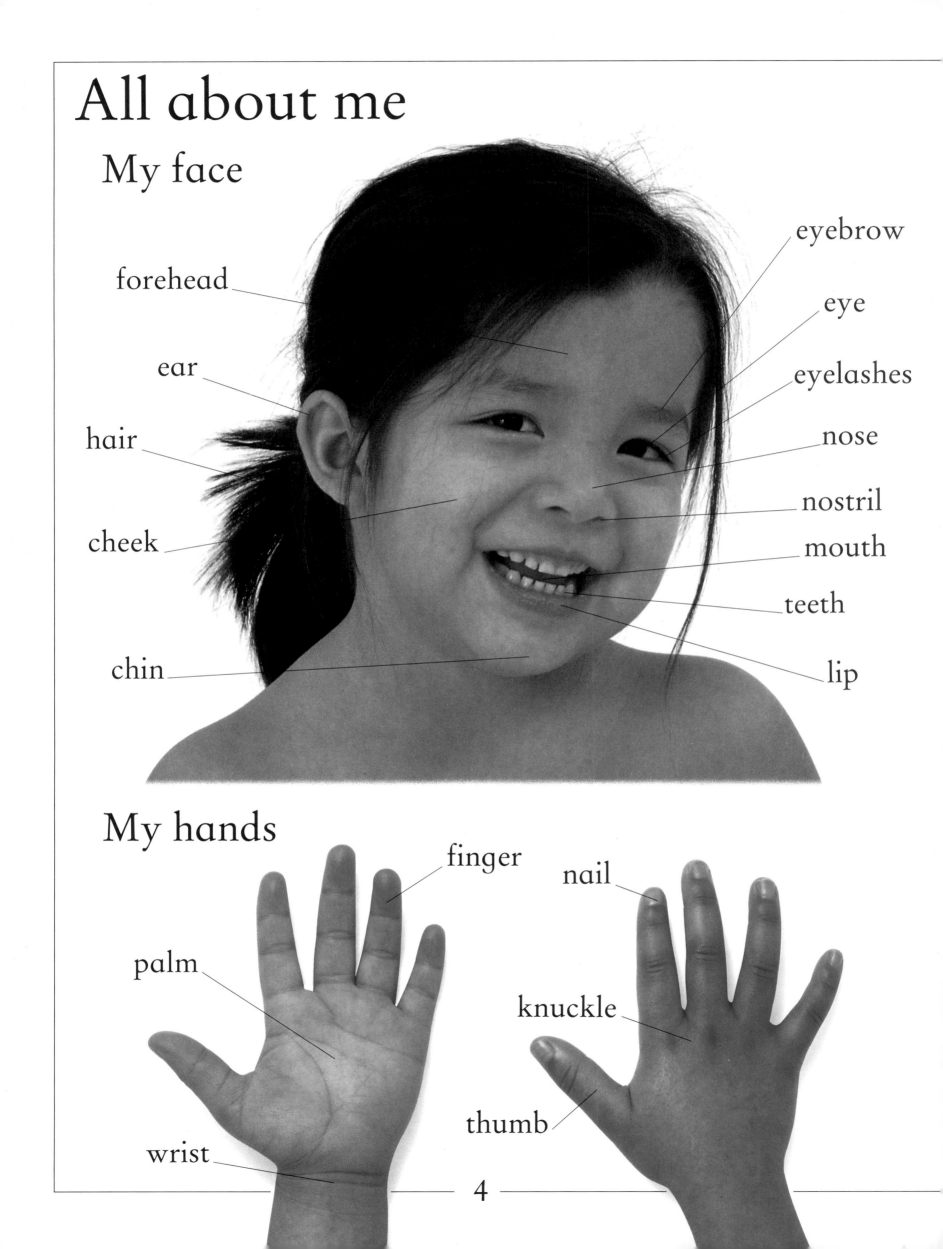

forehead

eyebrow

eye

ear

eyelashes

hair

nose

nostril

cheek

mouth

teeth

chin

lip

My hands

finger

nail

palm

knuckle

wrist

thumb

My body

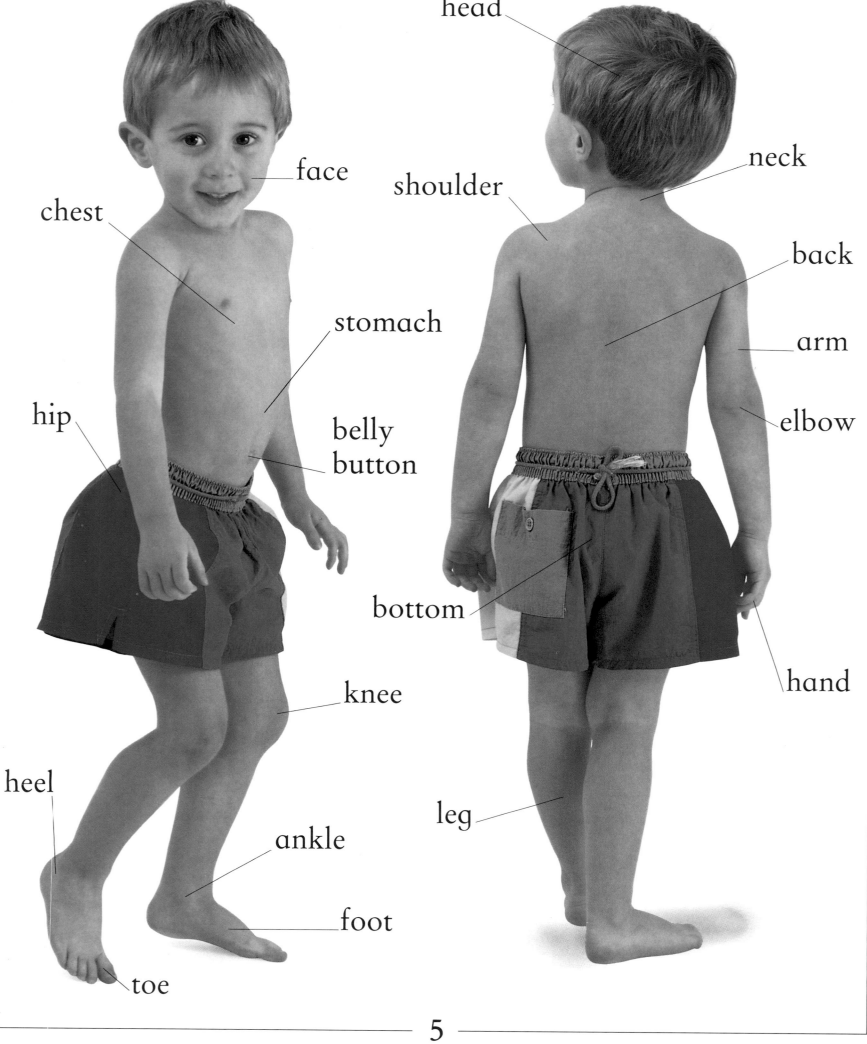

head

neck

shoulder

back

arm

elbow

face

chest

stomach

hip

belly
button

bottom

hand

knee

heel

leg

ankle

foot

toe

My clothes

buttons

buckle

belt

jacket

pants

sweater

suspenders

jeans

overalls

straw hat

wool hat

briefs

T-shirt

pajamas

beads

shorts

watch

socks

slippers

shoes

sneakers

sandals

underpants

undershirt

6

sweatshirt

hanger

slip

coat

sweatpants

skirt

nightgown

scarf

blouse

dress

bathrobe

cap

snowsuit

raincoat

mittens

boots

gloves

umbrella

pullover

tights

7

At home

attic

basement

shutters

gutter

drainpipe

balcony

ceiling

bed

bedroom

fireplace

bush

living room

couch

banister

stove

staircase

wallpaper

carpeting

floor

bathtub bathroom

kitchen

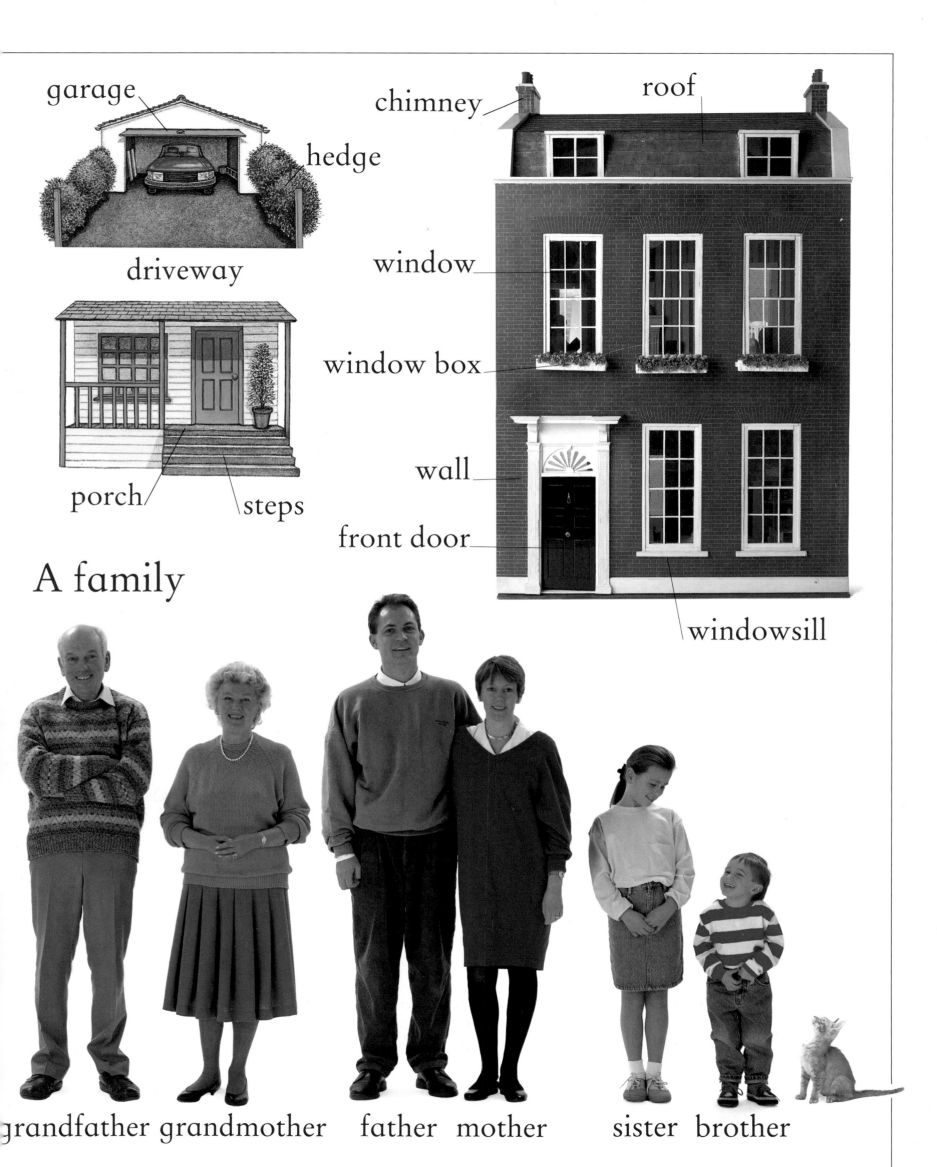

garage

hedge

driveway

chimney

roof

window

window box

wall

front door

windowsill

porch

steps

A family

grandfather grandmother father mother sister brother

9

Around the house

telephone

hairdryer

couch

curtains

radiator

picture

vacuum cleaner

radio

turntable

book

stool

bookshelf

doormat

sewing machine

armchair

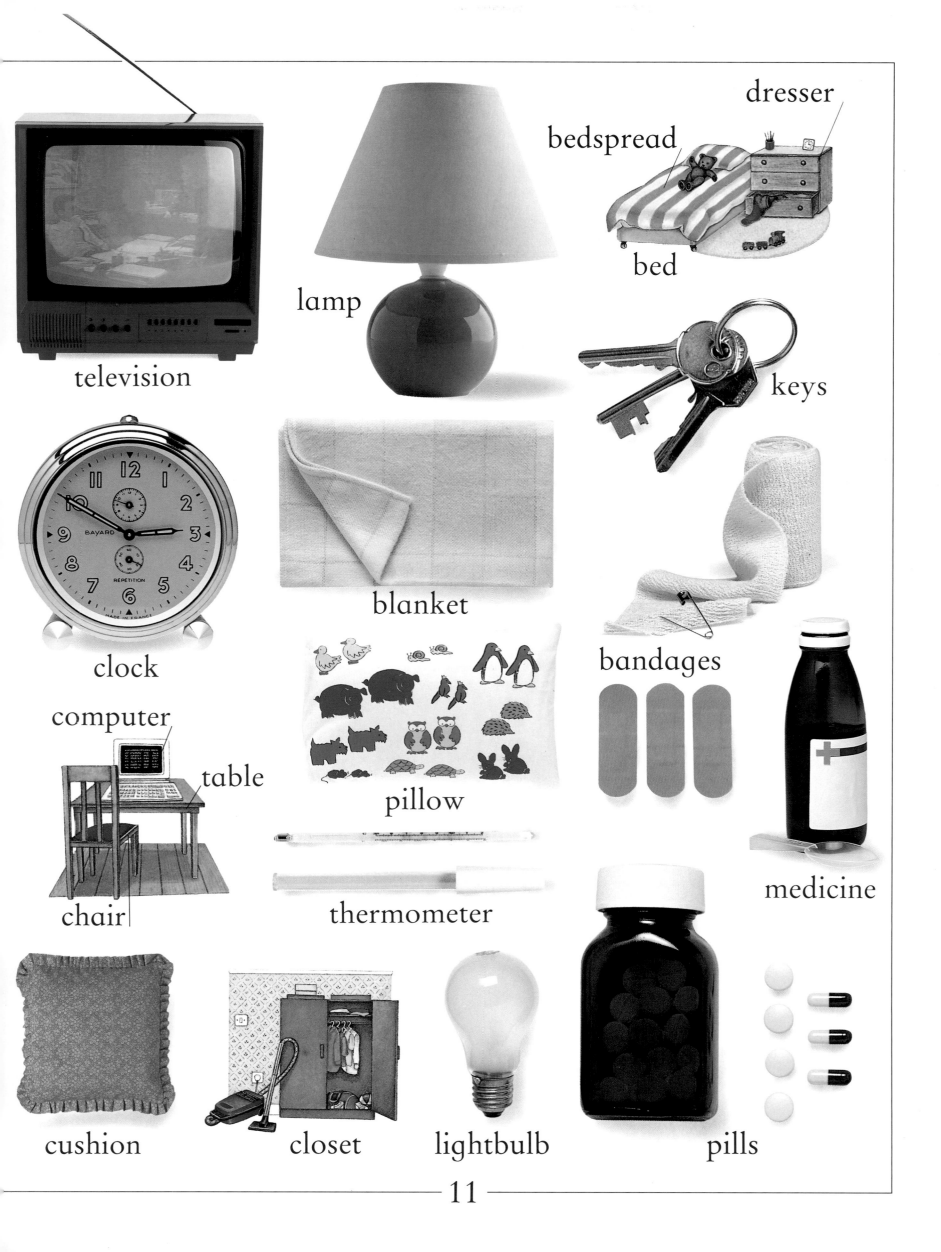

television

lamp

bedspread

dresser

bed

keys

clock

blanket

bandages

medicine

computer

table

pillow

chair

thermometer

cushion

closet

lightbulb

pills

In the kitchen

rolling pin

frying pan

rubber gloves

egg cup

brush

dustpan

electric mixer

pitcher

refrigerator

oven

stove

plate

place mat

napkin

oven mitt

knife

fork

apron

broom

strainer

spoon

12

kettle

washing machine

mop

glass

cereal bowl

mug

colander

cup

saucer

matches

teapot

cake pan

saucepan

sink

dish drainer

garbage can

cupboard

cookie cutters

ironing board

mixing bowl

high chair

iron

13

Things to eat and drink

tarts

apples

hot dogs

honey

sugar

pears

salad

almonds

peas

corn on the cob

tomatoes

cookies

pizza

hamburger

french fries

milk

juice

butter

sandwich

14

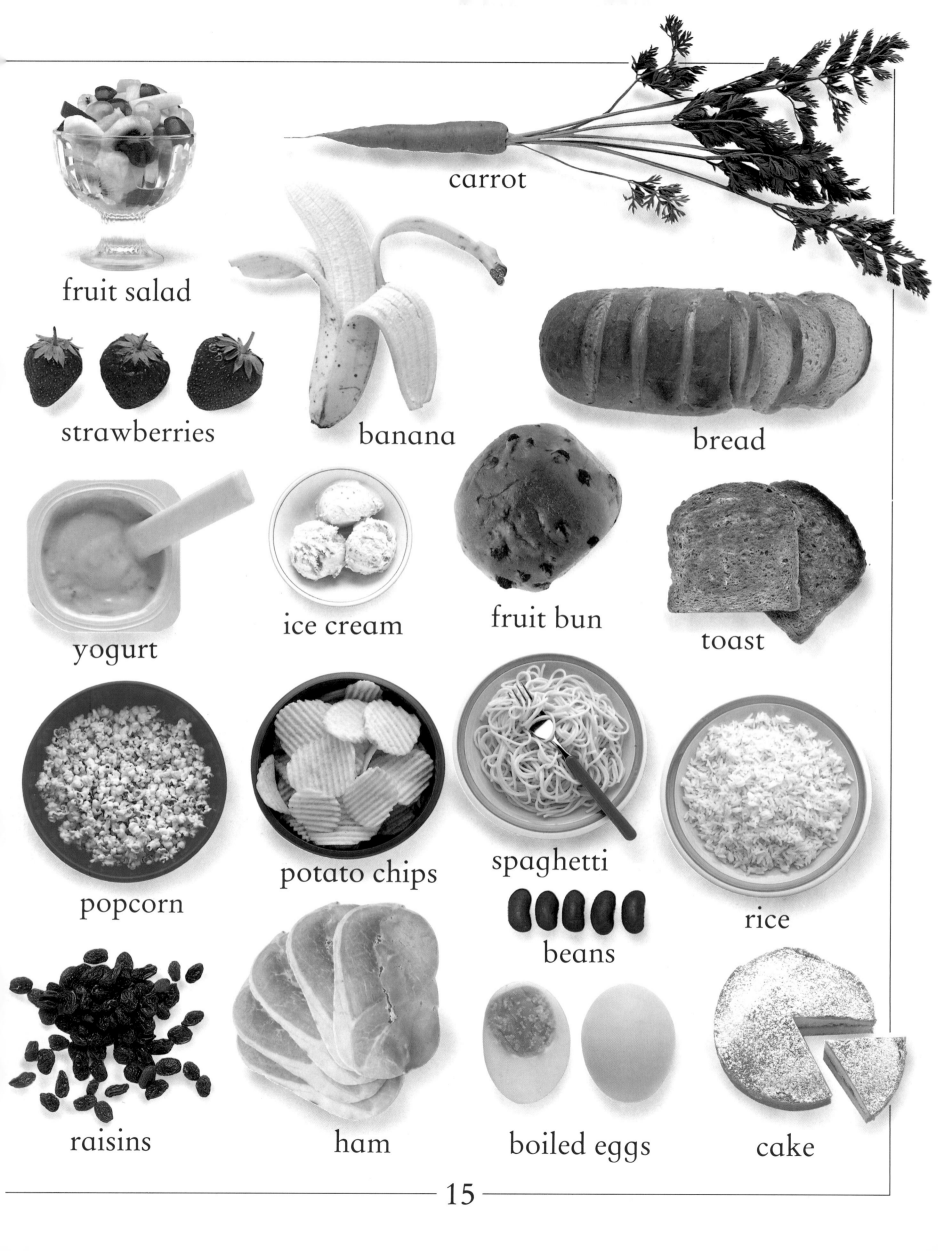

fruit salad

carrot

strawberries

banana

bread

yogurt

ice cream

fruit bun

toast

popcorn

potato chips

spaghetti

rice

beans

raisins

ham

boiled eggs

cake

In the bathroom

toothpaste

toothbrush

cotton balls

cosmetics bag

faucet

sponges

headband

towel

sink

ribbons

comb

hairbrush

shampoo

deodorant

perfume

barrette

water

bathtub

bath mat

talcum powder

potty

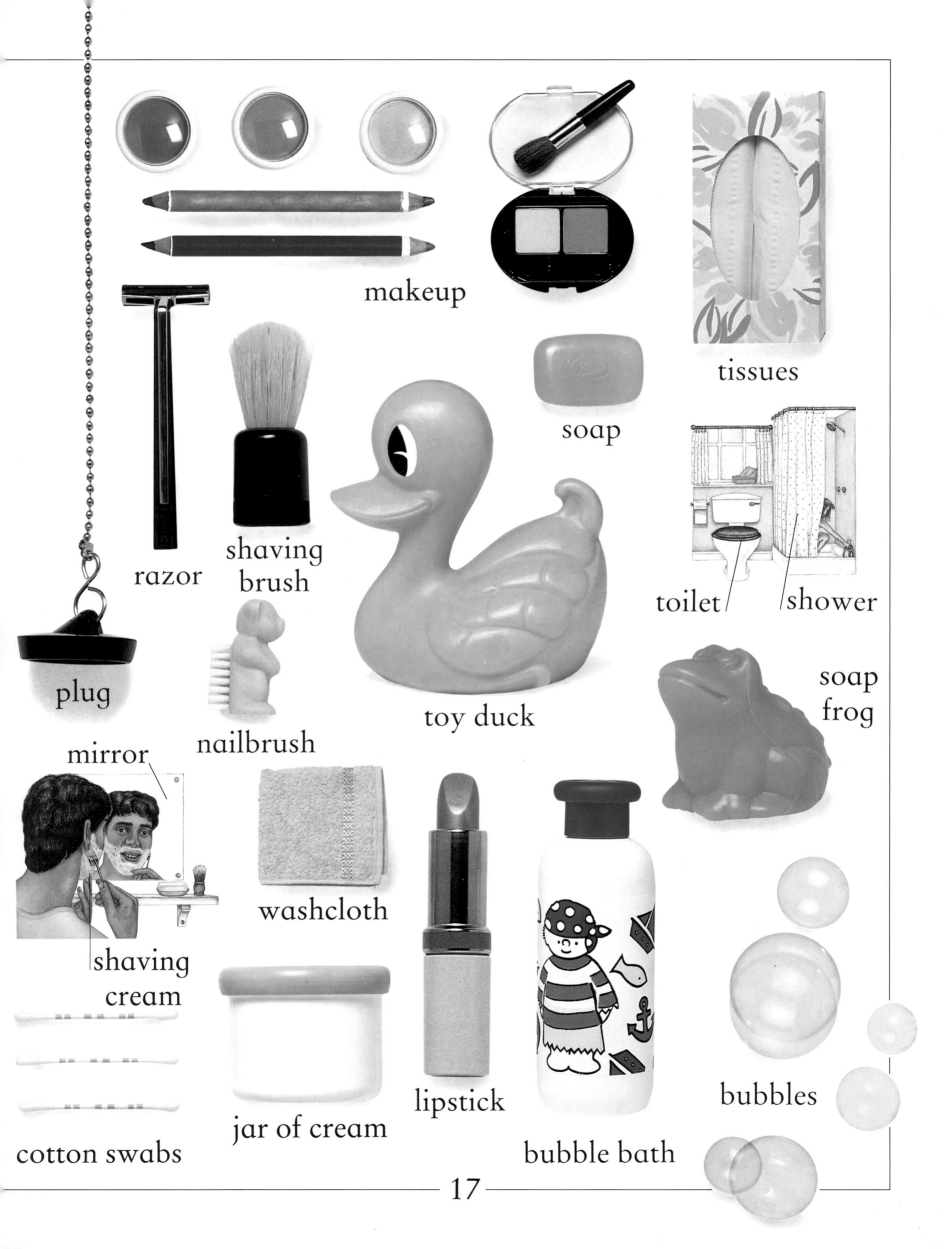

makeup

tissues

soap

razor

shaving
brush

toilet   shower

plug

nailbrush

toy duck

soap
frog

mirror

washcloth

shaving
cream

lipstick

bubbles

cotton swabs

jar of cream

bubble bath

17

In the garden

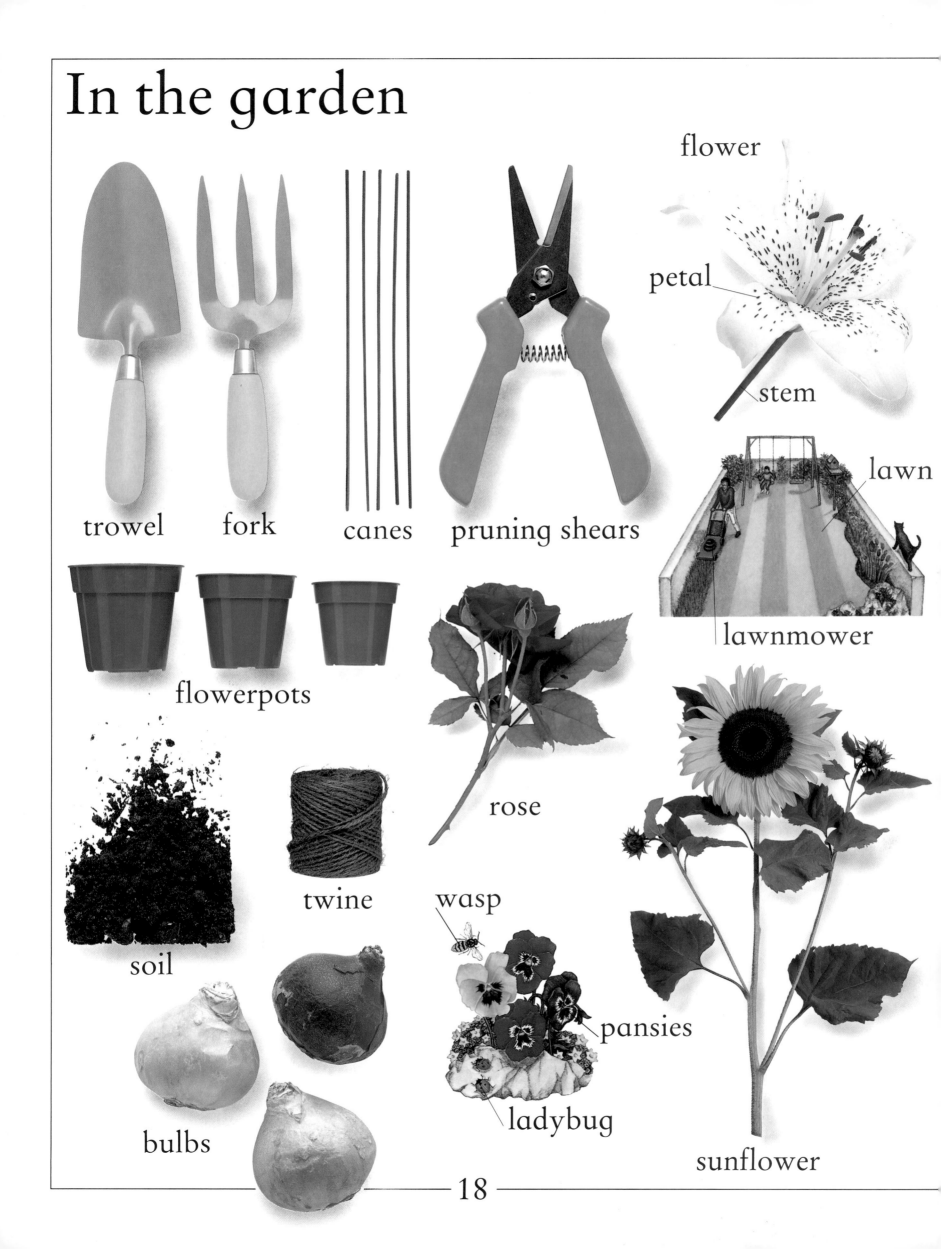

trowel

fork

canes

pruning shears

flower

petal

stem

lawn

lawnmower

flowerpots

rose

soil

twine

wasp

pansies

ladybug

bulbs

sunflower

18

seedlings

seed tray

daffodils

butterfly

bee

watering can

seeds

spade

rake

potted plant

tulips

weeds

ants

grass

worms

wheelbarrow

greenhouse

nasturtium plant

snail

hose

In the toolshed

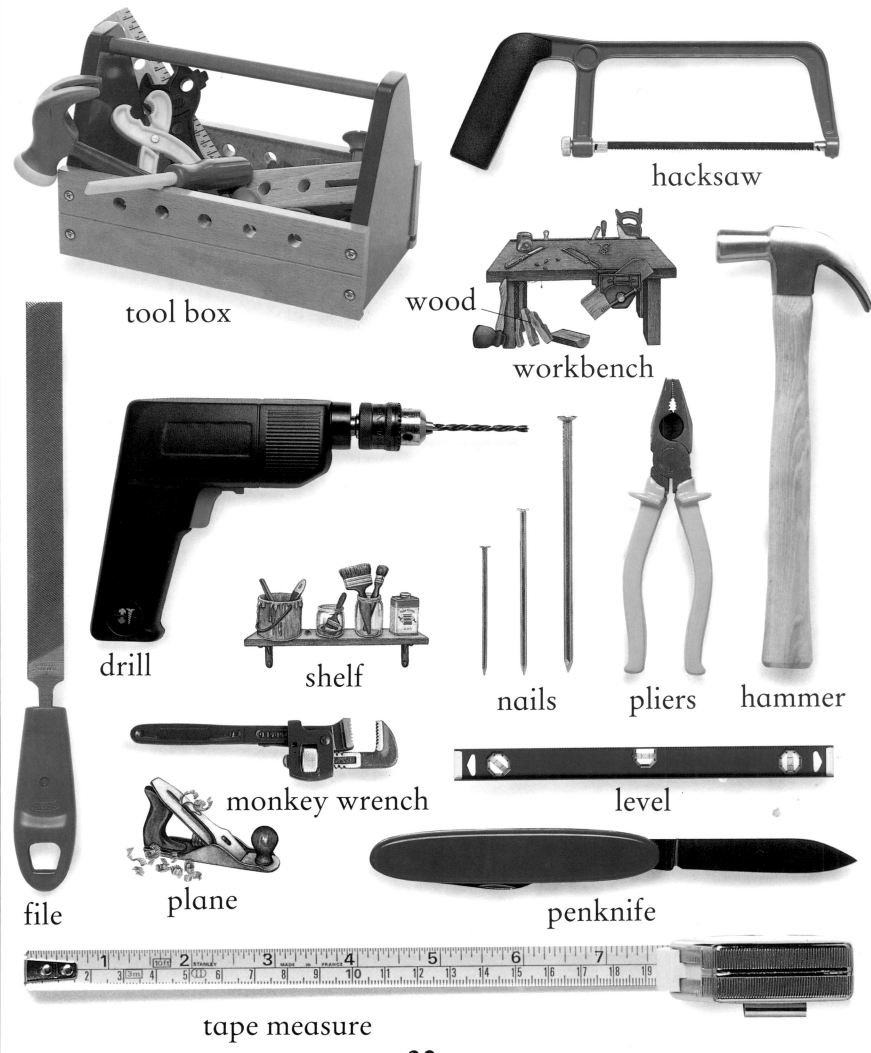

tool box

hacksaw

wood

workbench

file

drill

shelf

nails

pliers

hammer

monkey wrench

level

plane

penknife

tape measure

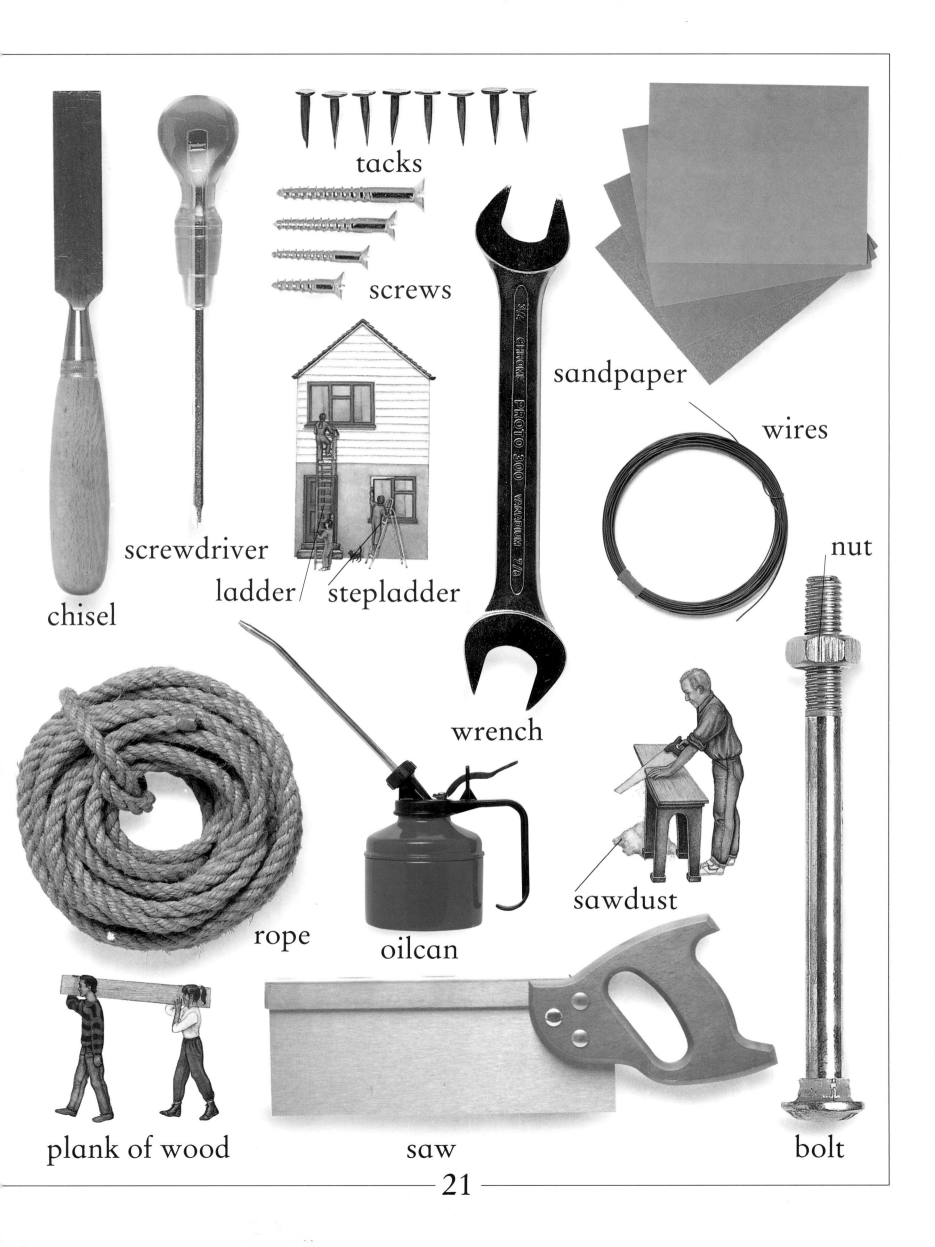

tacks

screws

sandpaper

wires

chisel

screwdriver

ladder   stepladder

nut

wrench

rope

oilcan

sawdust

plank of wood

saw

bolt

Going out

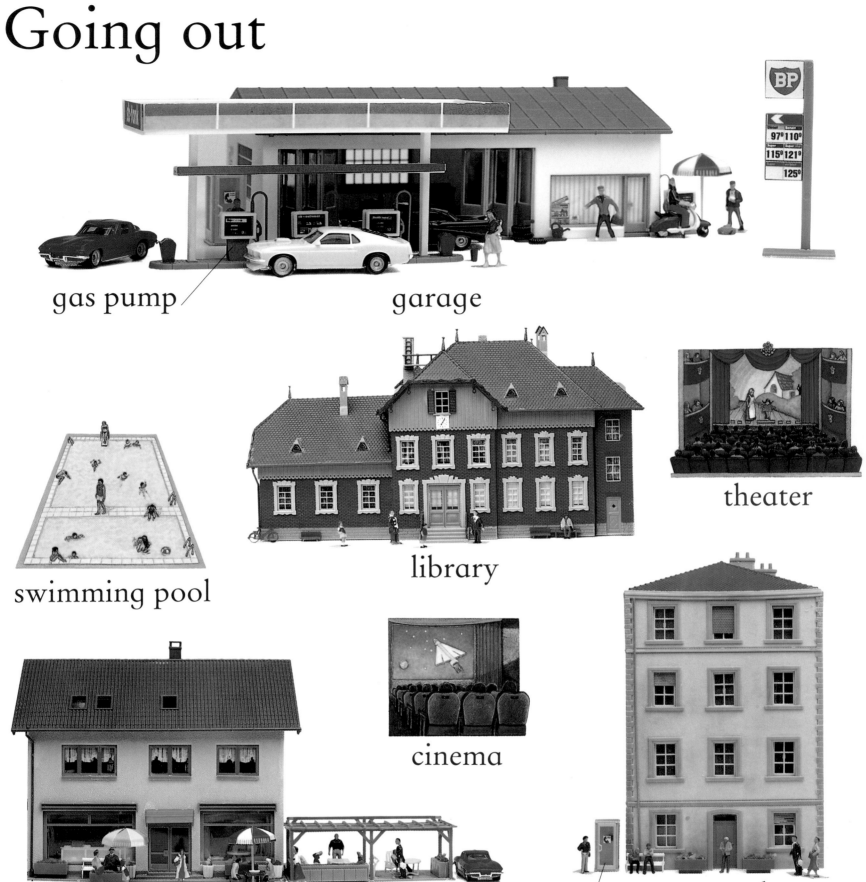

gas pump

garage

swimming pool

library

theater

restaurant

cinema

telephone booth

apartment house

stalls

outdoor market

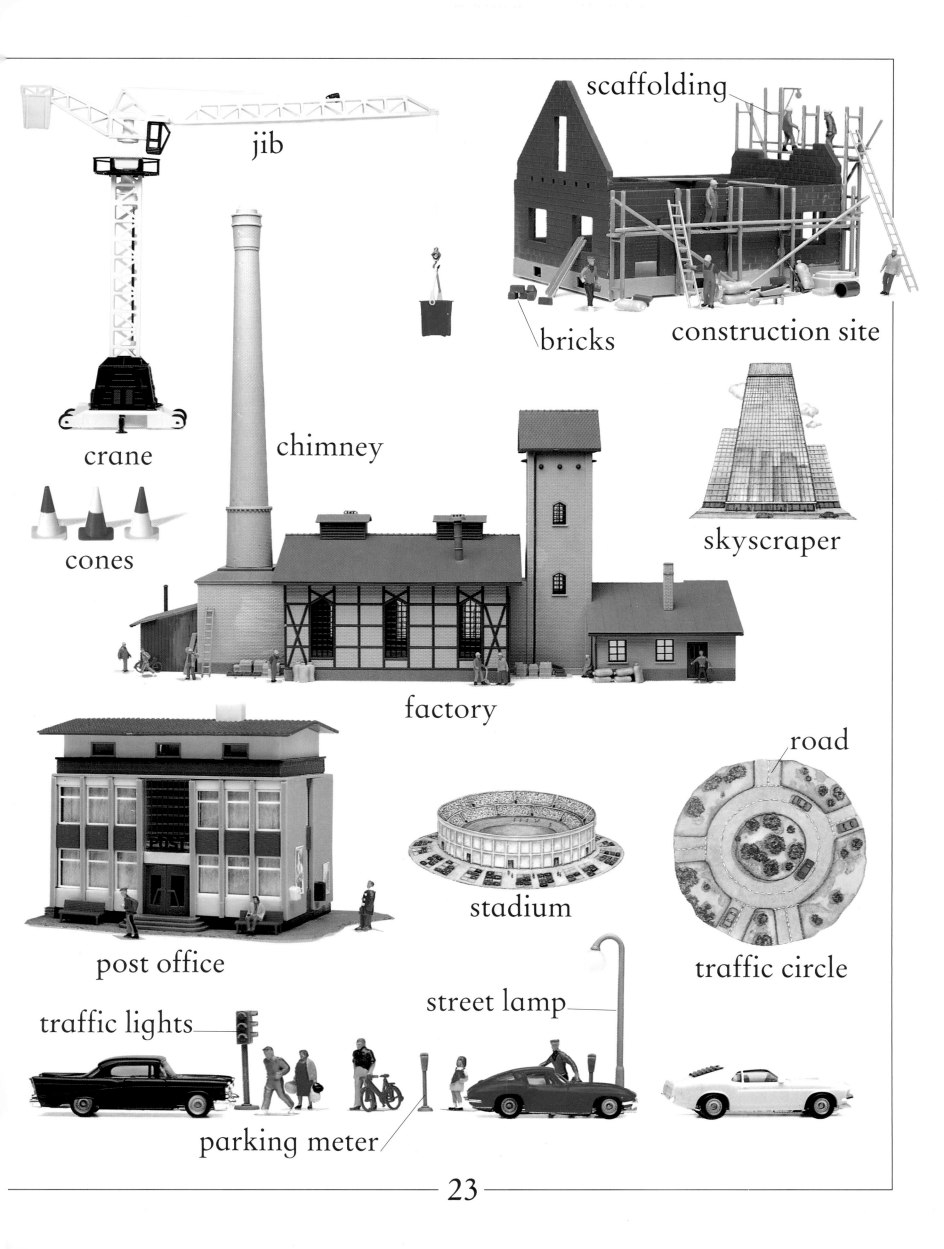

jib

scaffolding

bricks

construction site

crane

chimney

cones

skyscraper

factory

road

post office

stadium

traffic circle

street lamp

traffic lights

parking meter

At the park

picnic basket

picnic

statue

bench

fountain

flower bed

stroller

children

tricycle

kite

sandbox

roller skates

carousel

jump rope

skateboard

swan

cygnet

swing

jungle gym

seesaw

slide

pigeons

ice-cream truck

baby
carriage

lunch box

thermos

At the supermarket

basket

cereal

cooking oil

candy

dish soap

jam

flour

coffee

meat

fish

toilet paper

Fruit

grapes

peaches

cherries

pineapple

lemon

orange

raspberries

blueberries

chocolate

cans

shopping cart

detergent

cash register

bottles

cheese

checks

purse

money

box

cashier

checkout counter

paper bag

Vegetables

green beans

celery

pepper

onion

zucchini

cabbage

potatoes

cucumber

lettuce

Cars

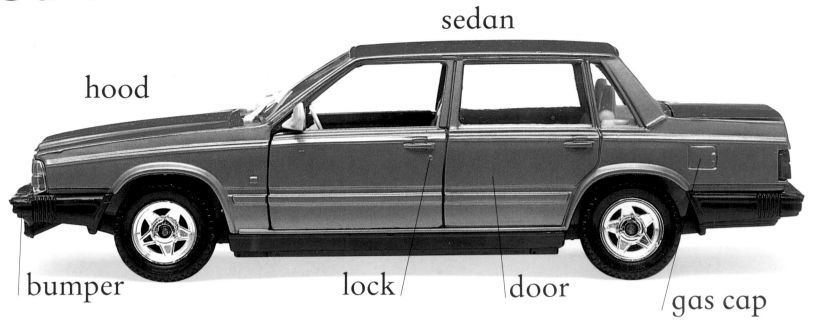

sedan

hood

bumper

lock

door

gas cap

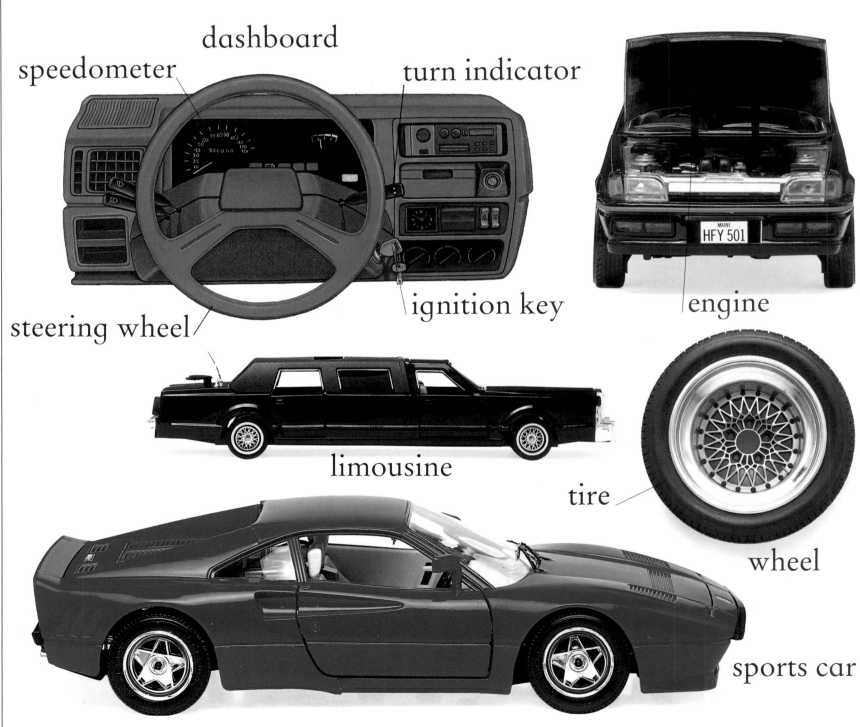

dashboard

speedometer

turn indicator

steering wheel

ignition key

engine

limousine

tire

wheel

sports car

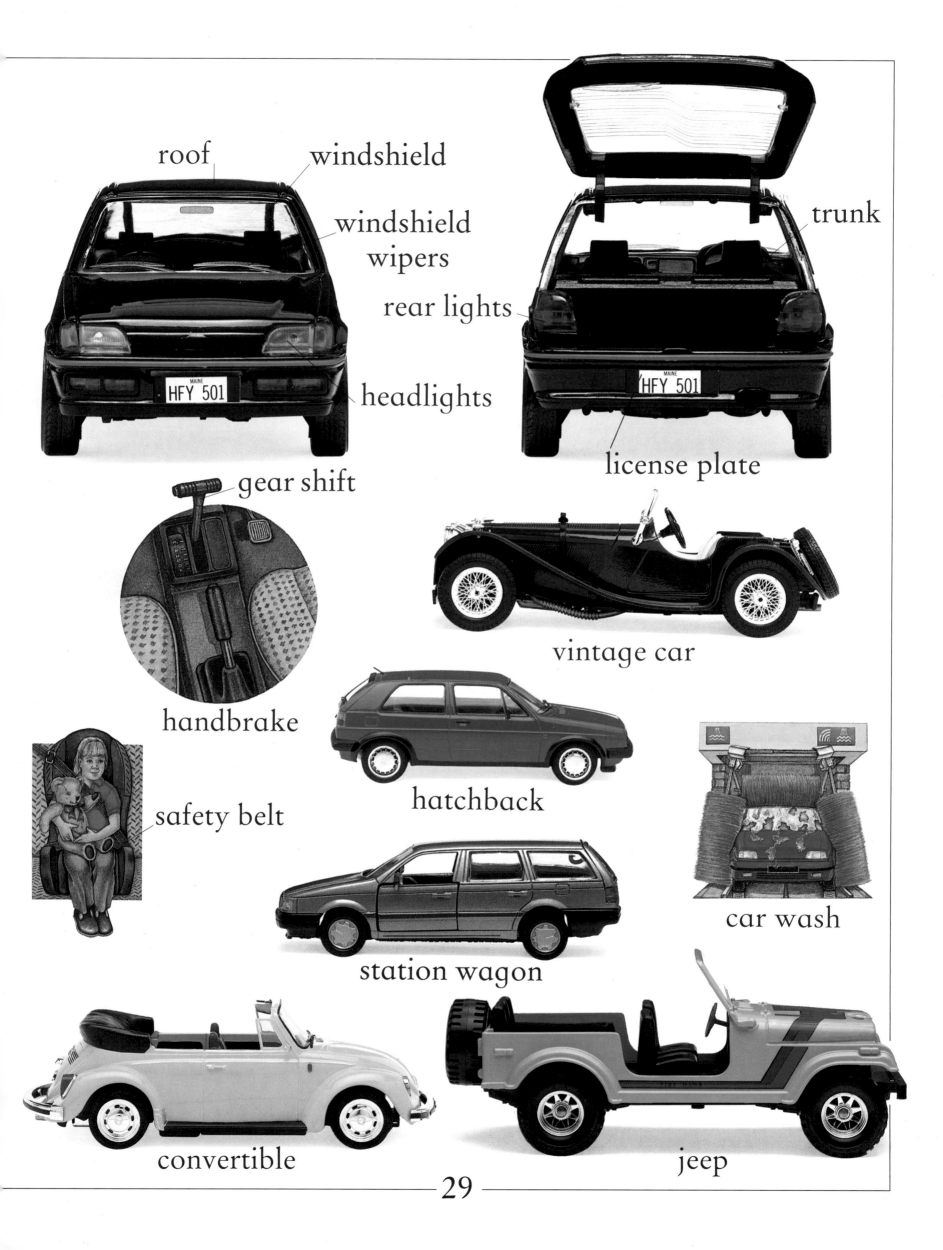

roof

windshield

windshield wipers

rear lights

headlights

trunk

license plate

gear shift

handbrake

vintage car

safety belt

hatchback

car wash

station wagon

convertible

jeep

29

Things that move

bicycle

digger

motor bike

car

car ferry

taxicab

truck

boat

blimp

bulldozer

parachutes

motorcycle

submarine

railway car

train tracks

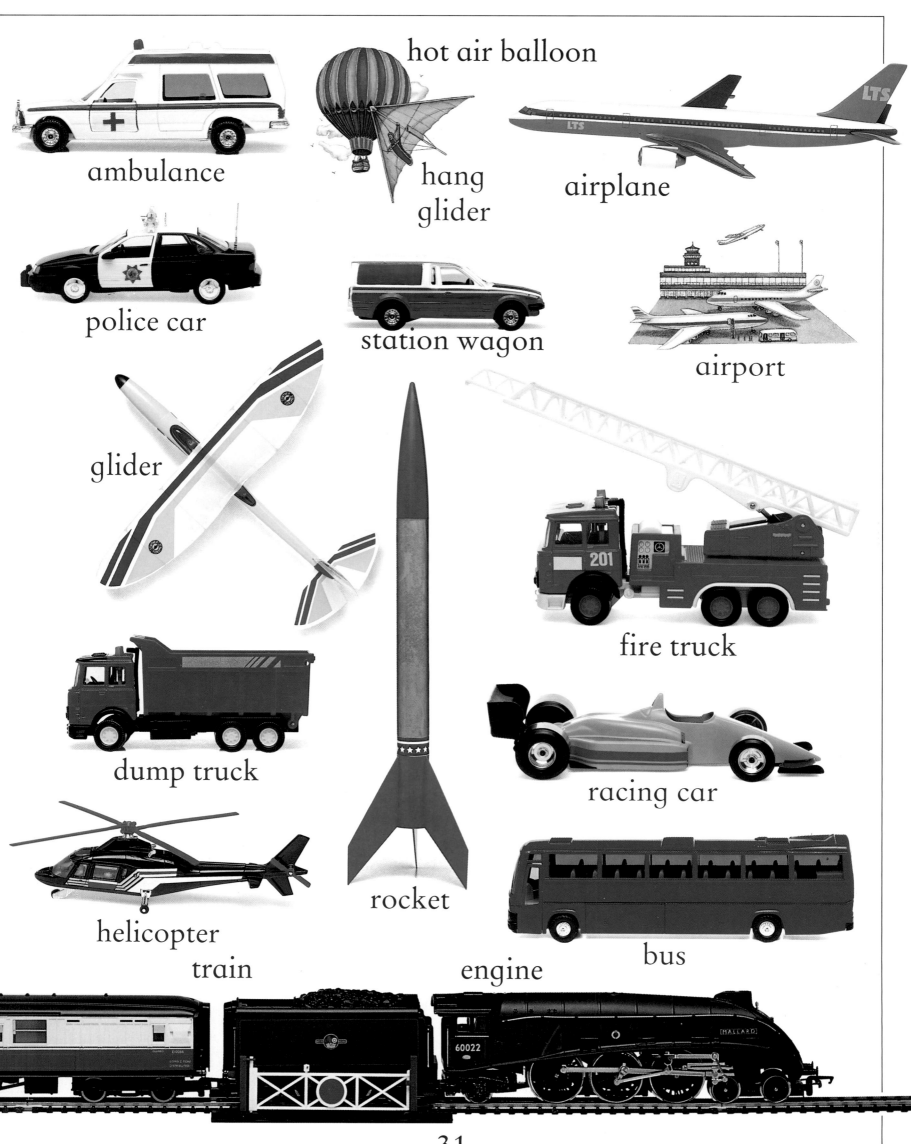

ambulance

hot air balloon

hang glider

airplane

police car

station wagon

airport

glider

fire truck

dump truck

racing car

rocket

helicopter

bus

train

engine

In the country

orchard

village

rabbit

dragonfly

waterlilies

stream

mountain

valley

lake

island

hills

bridge

river

ferns

toad

mushrooms

road

blackberries

fox

camper

tent

campsite

Wildflowers

waterfall

dandelion

buttercups

daisies

In the woods

tree

acorns

plums

pinecones

blossom

berries

fir needles

branch

squirrel

bird's eggs

bird

baby birds

trunk

bird's nest

owl

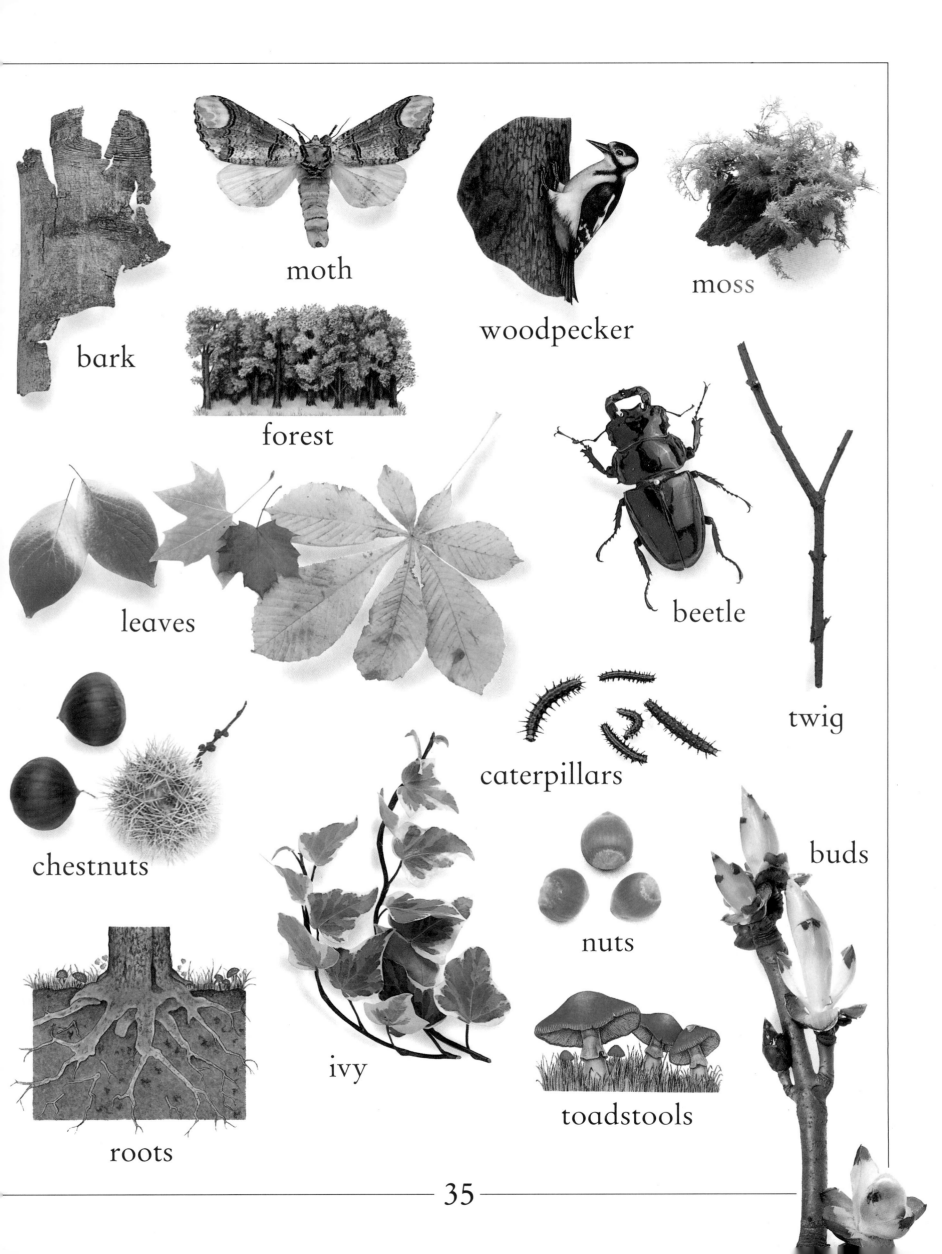

bark

moth

woodpecker

moss

forest

leaves

beetle

twig

chestnuts

caterpillars

buds

nuts

roots

ivy

toadstools

35

On the farm

farmyard

trough

horse

farmhouse

goose

field

fence

pig

piglets

lamb

sheep

goat

wheatfield

hay bale

pigsty

gate

tractor

trailer

bull

calf

cow

chicken coop

chick

chicken

stable

pond

rooster

dog

ducklings

duck

barn

combine harvester

plow

Pets

hamsters

shell

turtle

whiskers

parrots

beak

tadpoles

tail

cat

feathers

guinea pig

goldfish

aquarium

puppies

collar

leash

bone

fur

mouse

dog

paws

perch

canary

cage

kittens

basket

mane

hooves

pony

wing

claws

parakeet

39

At the zoo

crocodile

scales

pelican

leopard

peacock

kangaroo

horns

fin

dolphin

hippopotamus

gazelle

shark

tiger

chimpanzee

ostrich

giraffe

bear

lizard

rhinoceros

penguin

camel

panda

polar bear

buffalo

koala

tusk

trunk

elephant

lion

snake

zebra

anteater

41

My toys

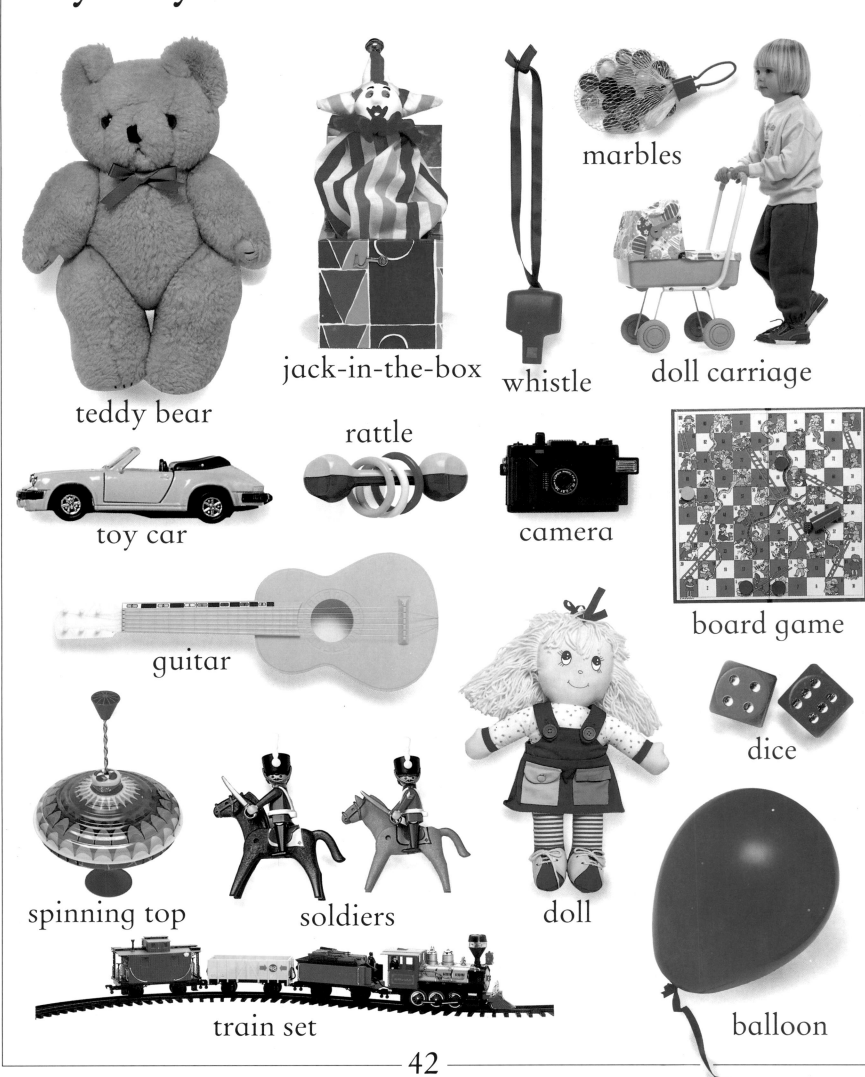

teddy bear

jack-in-the-box

whistle

marbles

doll carriage

rattle

toy car

camera

board game

guitar

spinning top

soldiers

doll

dice

balloon

train set

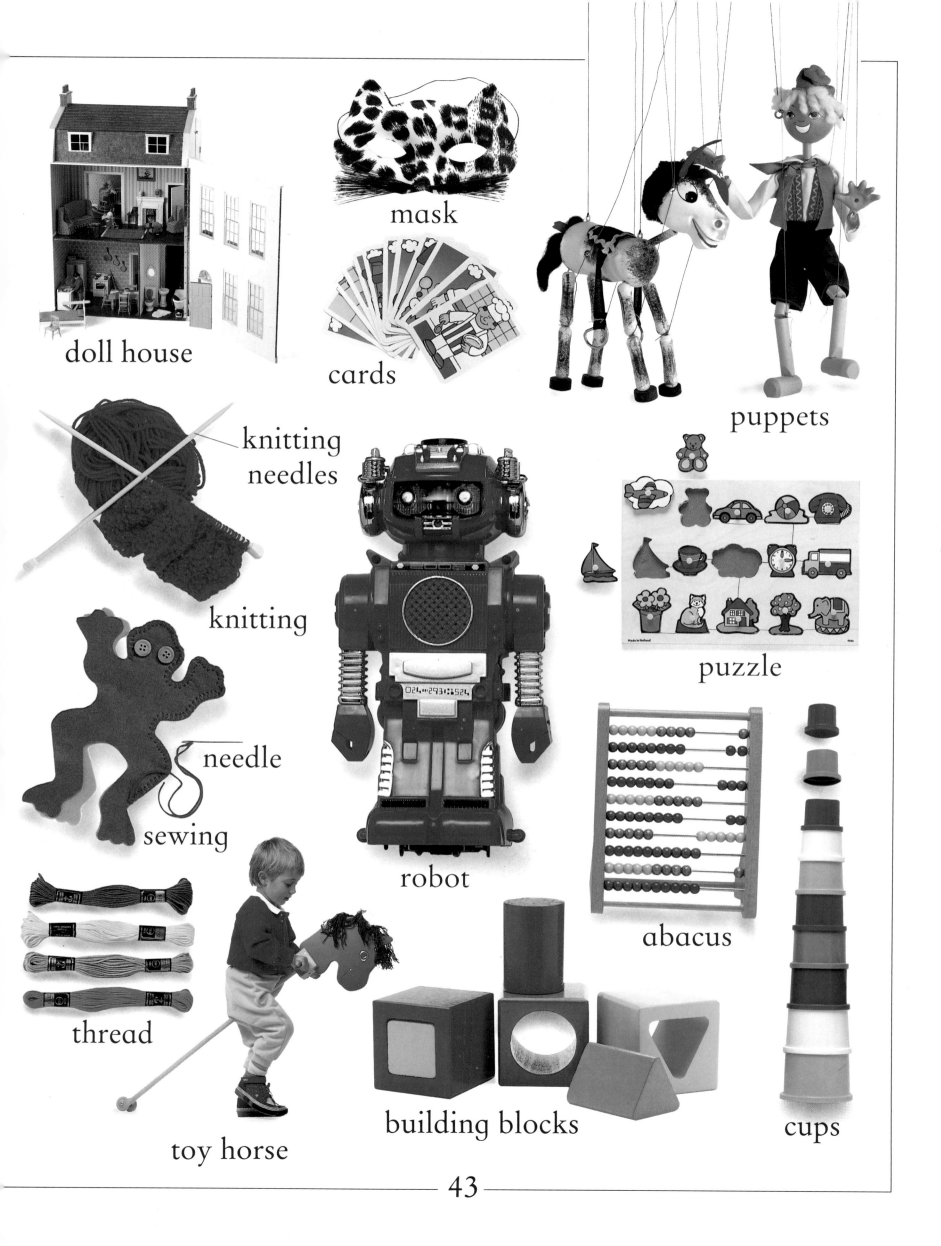

doll house

mask

cards

puppets

knitting needles

knitting

needle

sewing

thread

toy horse

robot

puzzle

abacus

building blocks

cups

Going to school

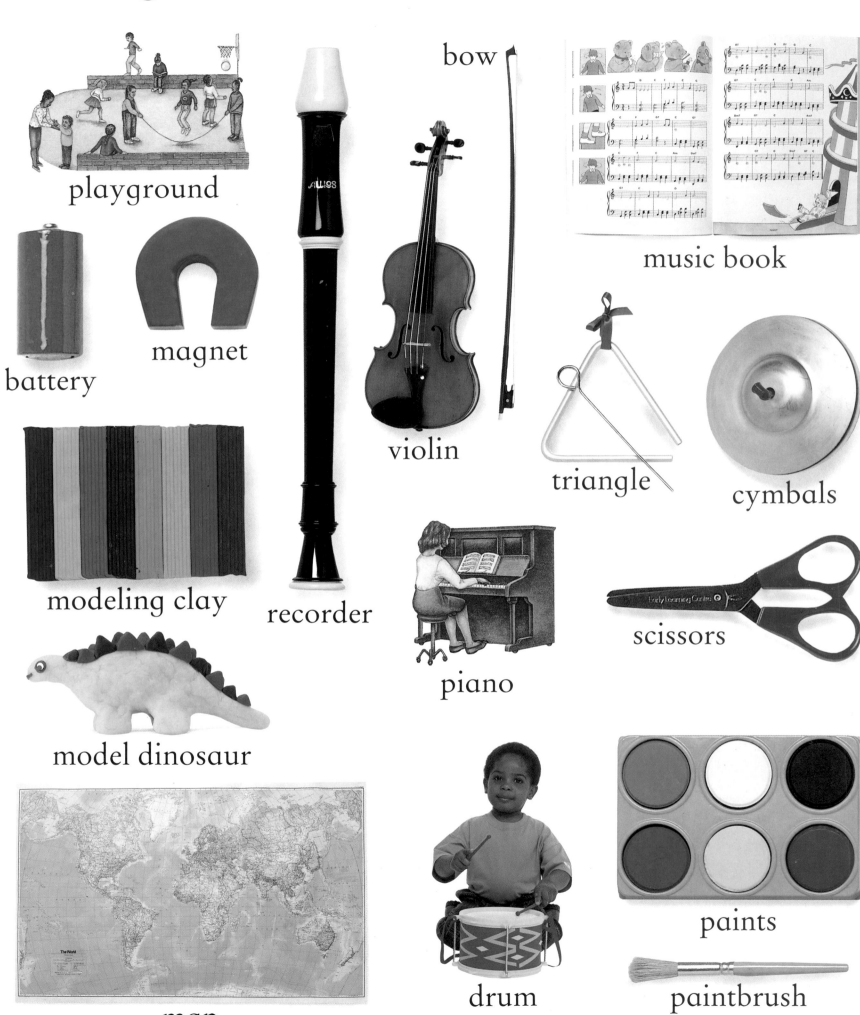

playground

battery

magnet

modeling clay

model dinosaur

recorder

bow

violin

music book

triangle

cymbals

piano

scissors

paints

paintbrush

drum

map

letters

teacher

writing

books

globe

glue

chalk

blackboard

12345678910
numbers

pencil

eraser

paper

drawing

calendar

easel

painting

ruler

crayons

At the seaside

flag

sandcastle

pinwheel

pebbles

rocks

deck chair

waves

fish

float

cliffs

sea

beach

shell

seaweed

sand

harbor

starfish

water wings

sunglasses

ice-cream
cone

lighthouse

beach umbrella

seagulls

crab

swimsuit

beach ball

shovel

handle

sun hat

sail

pail

tidal pool

sailboat

Time, weather, and seasons

Time

daytime

breakfast time

playtime

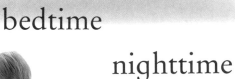
bedtime

nighttime

lunchtime

suppertime

Days of the week

Sunday	Thursday
Monday	Friday
Tuesday	Saturday
Wednesday	

Months of the year

January	May	September
February	June	October
March	July	November
April	August	December

Weather

sun

cloud

rainbow

raindrops

rainy

puddle

windy

snowman

snow

Seasons

spring

summer

fall

winter

Sports

helmet

football game

ice skate

skating

football

birdies

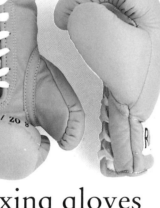

boxing gloves

darts

skiing

skis

badminton racket

fishing net

horseback riding

fishing rod

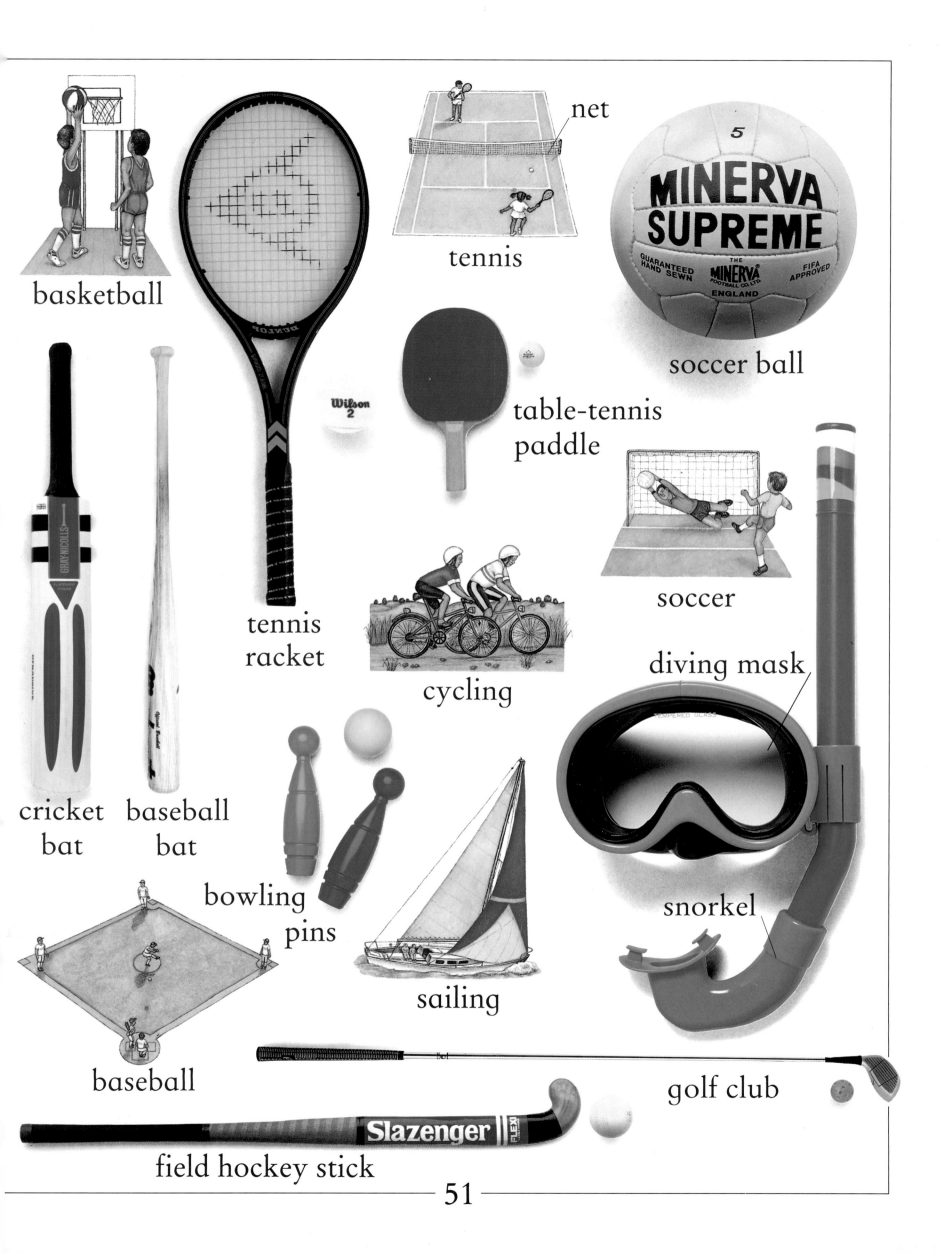

basketball

net

tennis

MINERVA SUPREME

soccer ball

tennis racket

Wilson 2

table-tennis paddle

soccer

cycling

diving mask

cricket bat

baseball bat

bowling pins

sailing

snorkel

baseball

field hockey stick

Slazenger FLEXI

golf club

51

Actions

reading

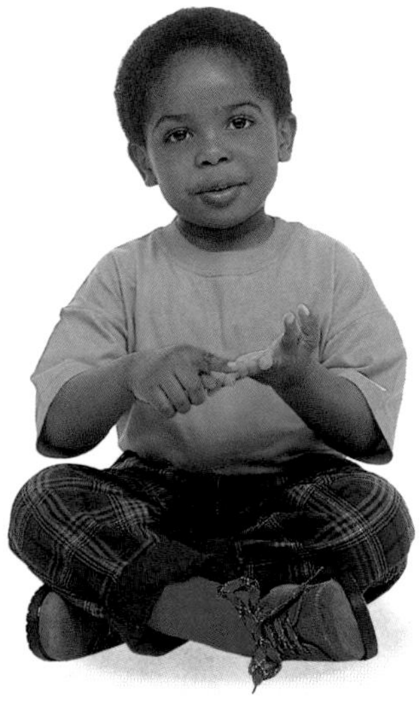

counting

eating

drinking

picking up

hugging

crying

sweeping

giving   taking

pushing

pulling

looking

whispering

shouting

listening

talking

pointing

standing

sitting

laughing

smiling

kissing

running

walking

carrying

sleeping

lying down

crawling

53

Playtime

playing

skipping

kicking

hitting

climbing

building

dancing

chasing

hopping

falling over

jumping

blowing   throwing   catching   hiding   riding

Storytime

chief

dragon

armor

knight

reindeer

sleigh

Santa Claus

dinosaur

cowboy

fairy

magic wand

pirate

crown

cloak

monster

king

queen

witch

sword

prince

princess

wizard

castle

giant

beanstalk

broomstick

pumpkin

Colors, shapes, and numbers

Colors

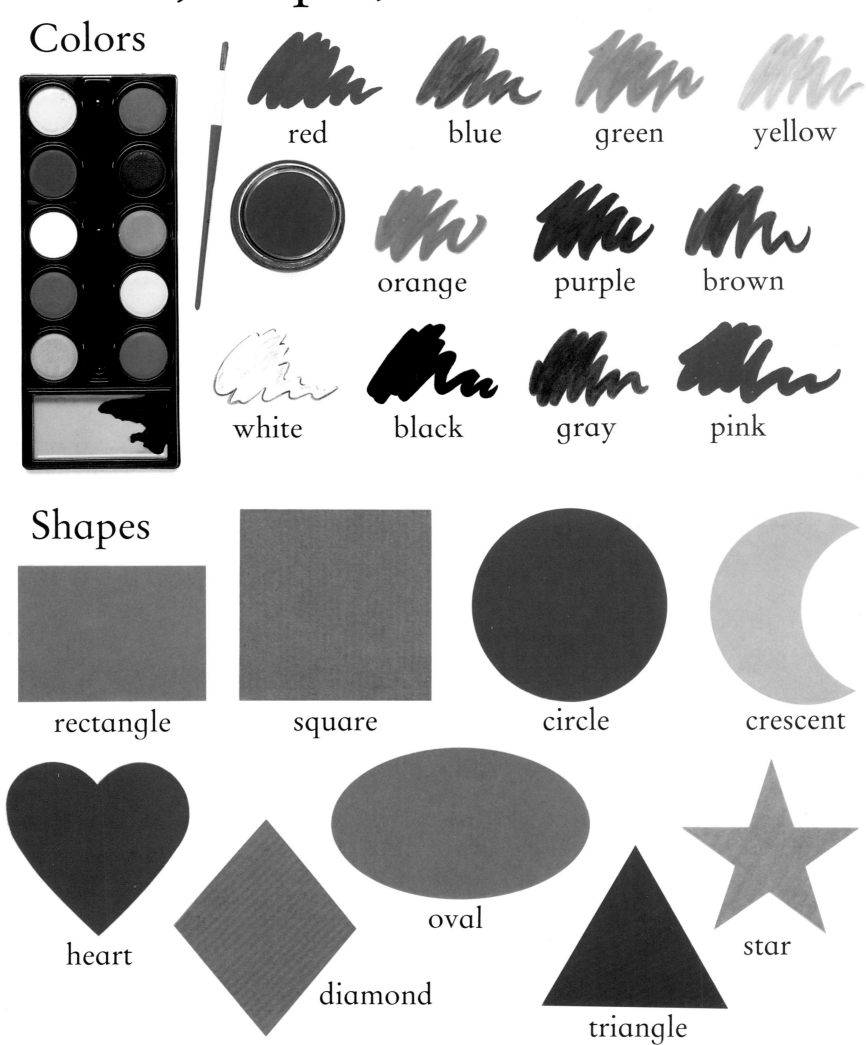

red

blue

green

yellow

orange

purple

brown

white

black

gray

pink

Shapes

rectangle

square

circle

crescent

heart

diamond

oval

triangle

star

Numbers

1	2	3	4	5	6	7
one	two	three	four	five	six	seven

8	9	10	11	12
eight	nine	ten	eleven	twelve

13	14	15	16
thirteen	fourteen	fifteen	sixteen

17	18	19	20
seventeen	eighteen	nineteen	twenty

Positions

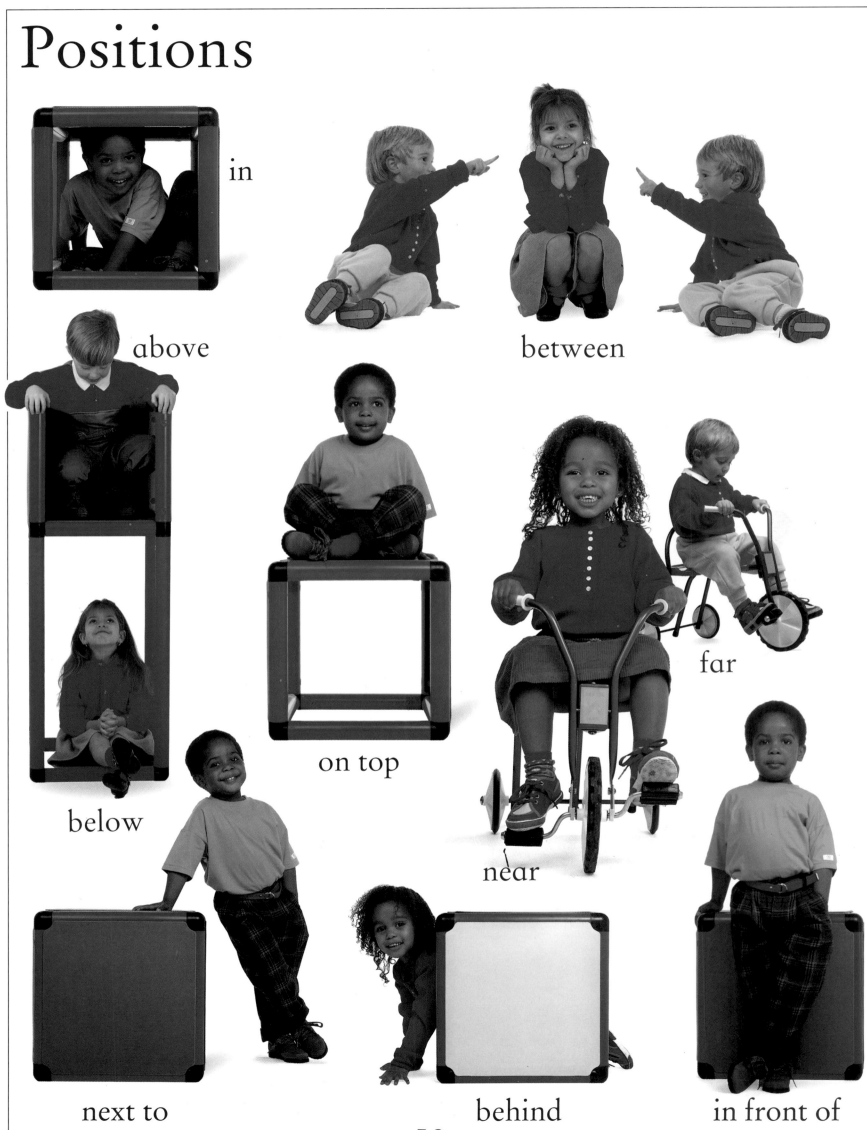

in

between

above

below

on top

far

near

next to

behind

in front of

up

down

top

on

off

over

under

bottom

fourth   third   second   first

59

Opposites

sad

happy

smooth

rough

thin

fat

fast

soft

hard

awake

slow

asleep

full

empty

wet

dry

left

big

little

open

shut

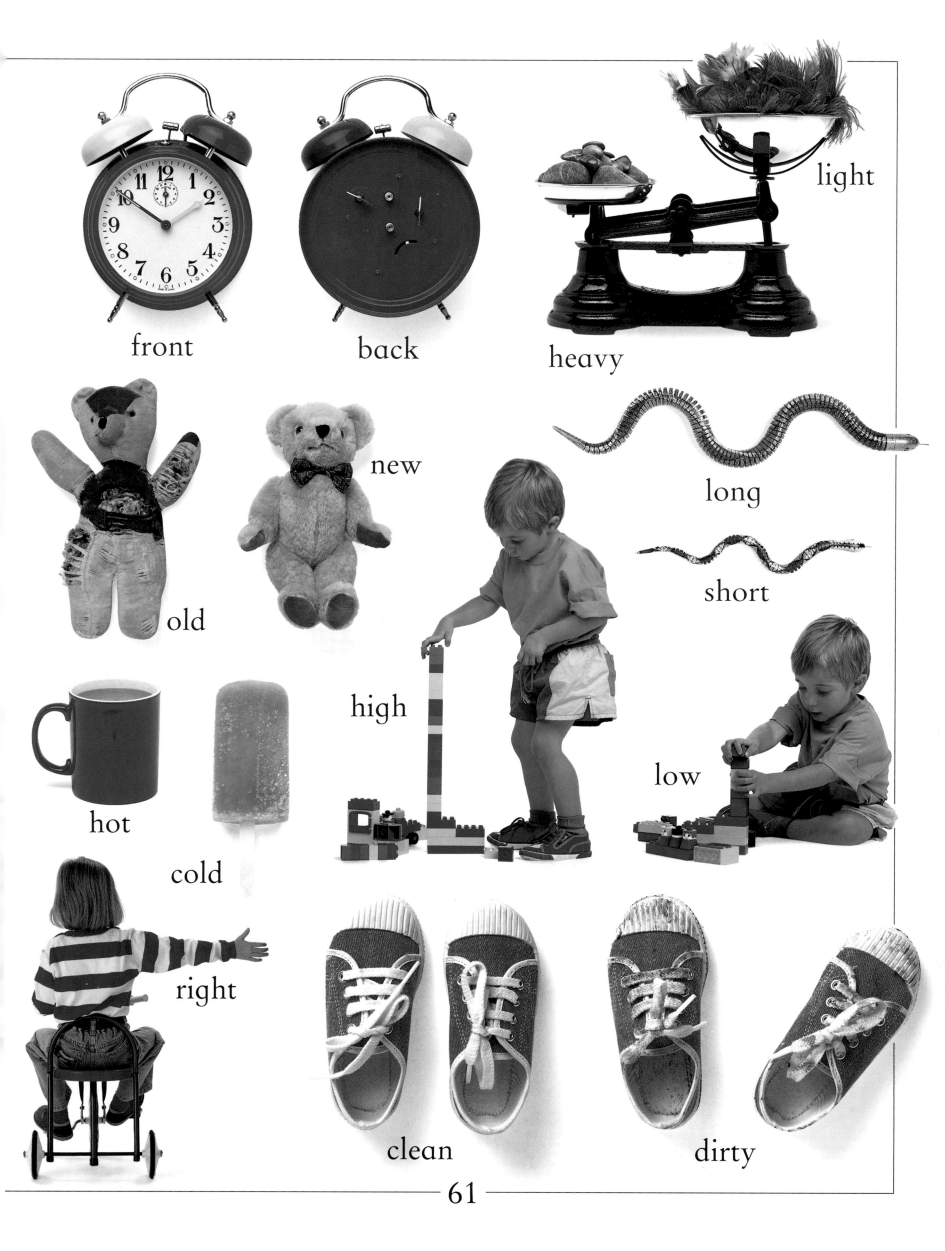

front

back

light

heavy

old

new

long

short

high

low

hot

cold

right

clean

dirty

Index

Abacus ...43
above ...58
acorns ...34
airplane ...31
airport ...31
almonds ...14
ambulance ...31
ankle ...5
anteater ...41
ants ...19
apartment house ...22
apples ...14
April ...48
apron ...12
aquarium ...38
arm ...5
armchair ...10
armor ...55
asleep ...60
attic ...8
August ...48
awake ...60

Baby birds ...34
baby carriage ...25
back ...5, 61
badminton racket ...50
balcony ...8
balloon ...42
banana ...15
bandages ...11
banister ...8
bark ...35
barn ...37
barrette ...16
baseball ...51
baseball bat ...51
basement ...8
basket ...26, 39
basketball ...51
bath mat ...16
bathrobe ...7
bathroom ...8
bathtub ...8, 16
battery ...44
beach ...46
beach ball ...47
beach umbrella ...47
beads ...6
beak ...38
beans ...15
beanstalk ...55
bear ...40
bed ...8, 11
bedroom ...8
bedspread ...11
bedtime ...48
bee ...19
beetle ...35
behind ...58
belly button ...5
below ...58
belt ...6
bench ...24
berries ...34
between ...58
bicycle ...30

big ...60
bird ...34
birdies ...50
bird's eggs ...34
bird's nest ...34
black ...56
blackberries ...33
blackboard ...45
blanket ...11
blimp ...30
blossom ...34
blouse ...7
blowing ...54
blue ...56
blueberries ...26
board game ...42
boat ...30
body ...5
boiled eggs ...15
bolt ...21
bone ...39
book ...10
books ...45
bookshelf ...10
boots ...7
bottles ...27
bottom ...5, 59
bow ...44
bowling pins ...51
box ...27
boxing gloves ...50
branch ...34
bread ...15
breakfast time ...48
bricks ...23
bridge ...32
briefs ...6
broom ...12
broomstick ...55
brother ...9
brown ...56
brush ...12
bubble bath ...17
bubbles ...17
buckle ...6
buds ...35
buffalo ...41
building ...54
building blocks ...43
bulbs ...18
bull ...37
bulldozer ...30
bumper ...28
bus ...31
bush ...8
butter ...14
buttercups ...33
butterfly ...19
buttons ...6

Cabbage ...27
cage ...39
cake ...15
cake pan ...13
calendar ...45
calf ...37
camel ...41

camera ...42
camper ...33
campsite ...33
canary ...39
candy ...26
canes ...18
cans ...27
cap ...7
car ...30
car ferry ...30
car wash ...29
cards ...43
carousel ...24
carpeting ...8
carrot ...15
carrying ...53
cashier ...27
cash register ...27
castle ...55
cat ...38
catching ...54
caterpillars ...35
ceiling ...8
celery ...27
cereal ...26
cereal bowl ...13
chair ...11
chalk ...45
chasing ...54
checkout counter ...27
checks ...27
cheek ...4
cheese ...27
cherries ...26
chest ...5
chestnuts ...35
chick ...37
chicken ...37
chicken coop ...37
chief ...55
children ...24
chimney ...9, 23
chimpanzee ...40
chin ...4
chisel ...21
chocolate ...27
cinema ...22
circle ...56
claws ...39
clean ...61
cliffs ...46
climbing ...54
cloak ...55
clock ...11
closet ...11
cloud ...49
coat ...7
coffee ...26
colander ...13
cold ...61
collar ...39
colors ...56
comb ...16
combine harvester ...37
computer ...11
cones ...23
construction site ...23

convertible ...29
cookie cutters ...13
cookies ...14
cooking oil ...26
corn on the cob ...14
cosmetics bag ...16
cotton balls ...16
cotton swabs ...17
couch ...8, 10
counting ...52
cow ...37
cowboy ...55
crab ...47
crane ...23
crawling ...53
crayons ...45
crescent ...56
cricket bat ...51
crocodile ...40
crown ...55
crying ...52
cucumber ...27
cup ...13
cupboard ...13
cups ...43
curtains ...10
cushion ...11
cycling ...51
cygnet ...25
cymbals ...44

Daffodils ...19
daisies ...33
dancing ...54
dandelion ...33
darts ...50
dashboard ...28
days ...48
daytime ...48
December ...48
deck chair ...46
deodorant ...16
detergent ...27
diamond ...56
dice ...42
digger ...30
dinosaur ...55
dirty ...61
dish drainer ...13
dish soap ...26
diving mask ...51
dog ...37, 39
doll ...42
doll carriage ...42
doll house ...43
dolphin ...40
door ...28
doormat ...10
down ...59
dragon ...55
dragonfly ...32
drainpipe ...8
drawing ...45
dress ...7
dresser ...11
drill ...20
drinking ...52

driveway ...9
drum ...44
dry ...60
duck ...37
ducklings ...37
dump truck ...31
dustpan ...12

Ear ...4
easel ...45
eating ...52
egg cup ...12
eight ...57
eighteen ...57
elbow ...5
electric mixer ...12
elephant ...41
eleven ...57
empty ...60
engine ...28, 31
eraser ...45
eye ...4
eyebrow ...4
eyelashes ...4

Face ...5
factory ...23
fairy ...55
fall ...49
falling over ...54
family ...9
far ...58
farmhouse ...36
farmyard ...36
fast ...60
fat ...60
father ...9
faucet ...16
feathers ...38
February ...48
fence ...36
ferns ...32
field ...36
field hockey stick ...51
fifteen ...57
file ...20
fin ...40
finger ...4
fir needles ...34
fire truck ...31
fireplace ...8
first ...59
fish ...26, 46
fishing net ...50
fishing rod ...50
five ...57
flag ...46
float ...46
floor ...8
flour ...26
flower ...18
flower bed ...24
flowerpots ...18
foot ...5
football ...50
football game ...50
forehead ...4

forest ...35
fork ...12, 18
fountain ...24
four ...57
fourteen ...57
fourth ...59
fox ...33
french fries ...14
Friday ...48
front ...61
front door ...9
fruit ...26
fruit bun ...15
fruit salad ...15
frying pan ...12
full ...60
fur ...39

Garage ...9, 22
garbage can ...13
gas cap ...28
gas pump ...22
gate ...36
gazelle ...40
gear shift ...29
giant ...55
giraffe ...40
giving ...52
glass ...13
glider ...31
globe ...45
gloves ...7
glue ...45
goat ...36
goldfish ...38
golf club ...51
goose ...36
grandfather ...9
grandmother ...9
grapes ...26
grass ...19
gray ...56
green ...56
green beans ...27
greenhouse ...19
guinea pig ...38
guitar ...42
gutter ...8

Hacksaw ...20
hair ...4
hairbrush ...16
hairdryer ...10
ham ...15
hamburger ...14
hammer ...20
hamsters ...38
hand ...5
handbrake ...29
handle ...47
hang glider ...31
hanger ...7
happy ...60
harbor ...46
hard ...60
hatchback ...29
hat, straw ...6
hat, sun ...47
hat, wool ...6
hay bale ...36
head ...5

headband ...16
headlights ...29
heart ...56
heavy ...61
hedge ...9
heel ...5
helicopter ...31
helmet ...50
hiding ...54
high ...61
high chair ...13
hills ...32
hip ...5
hippopotamus ...40
hitting ...54
honey ...14
hood ...28
hooves ...39
hopping ...54
horns ...40
horse ...36
horseback riding ...50
hose ...19
hot ...61
hot air balloon ...31
hot dogs ...14
hugging ...52

Ice cream ...15
ice-cream cone ...47
ice-cream truck ...25
ice skate ...50
ignition key ...28
in ...58
in front of ...58
iron ...13
ironing board ...13
island ...32
ivy ...35

Jack-in-the-box ...42
jacket ...6
jam ...26
January ...48
jar of cream ...17
jeans ...6
jeep ...29
jib ...23
juice ...14
July ...48
jump rope ...25
jumping ...54
June ...48
jungle gym ...25

Kangaroo ...40
kettle ...13
keys ...11
kicking ...54
king ...55
kissing ...53
kitchen ...8
kite ...24
kittens ...39
knee ...5
knife ...12
knight ...55
knitting ...43
knitting needles ...43
knuckle ...4
koala ...41

Ladder ...21
ladybug ...18
lake ...32
lamb ...36
lamp ...11
laughing ...53
lawn ...18
lawnmower ...18
leash ...39
leaves ...35
left ...60
leg ...5
lemon ...26
leopard ...40
letters ...45
lettuce ...27
level ...20
library ...22
license plate ...29
light ...61
lightbulb ...11
lighthouse ...47
limousine ...28
lion ...41
lip ...4
lipstick ...17
listening ...53
little ...60
living room ...8
lizard ...41
lock ...28
long ...61
looking ...52
low ...61
lunch box ...25
lunchtime ...48
lying down ...53

Magic wand ...55
magnet ...44
makeup ...17
mane ...39
map ...44
marbles ...42
March ...48
mask ...43
matches ...13
May ...48
meat ...26
medicine ...11
milk ...14
mirror ...17
mittens ...7
mixing bowl ...13
model dinosaur ...44
modeling clay ...44
Monday ...48
money ...27
monkey wrench ...20
monster ...55
months ...48
mop ...13
moss ...35
moth ...35
mother ...9
motor bike ...30
motorcycle ...30
mountain ...32
mouse ...39
mouth ...4
mug ...13

mushrooms ...33
music book ...44

Nail ...4
nailbrush ...17
nails ...20
napkin ...12
nasturtium plant ...19
near ...58
neck ...5
needle ...43
net ...51
new ...61
next to ...58
nightgown ...7
nighttime ...48
nine ...57
nineteen ...57
nose ...4
nostril ...4
November ...48
numbers ...45, 57
nut ...21
nuts ...35

October ...48
off ...59
oilcan ...21
old ...61
on ...59
on top ...58
one ...57
onion ...27
open ...60
orange ...26, 56
orchard ...32
ostrich ...40
outdoor market ...22
oval ...56
oven ...12
oven mitt ...12
over ...59
overalls ...6
owl ...34

Pail ...47
paintbrush ...44
painting ...45
paints ...44
pajamas ...6
palm ...4
panda ...41
pansies ...18
pants ...6
paper ...45
paper bag ...27
parachutes ...30
parakeet ...39
parking meter ...23
parrots ...38
paws ...39
peaches ...26
peacock ...40
pears ...14
peas ...14
pebbles ...46
pelican ...40
pencil ...45
penguin ...41
penknife ...20
pepper ...27

perch ...39
perfume ...16
petal ...18
piano ...44
picking up ...52
picnic ...24
picnic basket ...24
picture ...10
pig ...36
pigeons ...25
piglets ...36
pigsty ...36
pillow ...11
pills ...11
pineapple ...26
pinecones ...34
pink ...56
pinwheel ...46
pirate ...55
pitcher ...12
pizza ...14
place mat ...12
plane ...20
plank of wood ...21
plate ...12
playground ...44
playing ...54
playtime ...48
pliers ...20
plow ...37
plug ...17
plums ...34
pointing ...53
polar bear ...41
police car ...31
pond ...37
pony ...39
popcorn ...15
porch ...9
post office ...23
potato chips ...15
potatoes ...27
potted plant ...19
potty ...16
prince ...55
princess ...55
pruning shears ...18
puddle ...49
pulling ...52
pullover ...7
pumpkin ...55
puppets ...43
puppies ...38
purple ...56
purse ...27
pushing ...52
puzzle ...43

Queen ...55

Rabbit ...32
racing car ...31
radiator ...10
radio ...10
railway car ...30
rainbow ...49
raincoat ...7
raindrops ...49
rainy ...49
raisins ...15
rake ...19

raspberries ...26
rattle ...42
razor ...17
reading ...52
rear lights ...29
recorder ...44
rectangle ...56
red ...56
refrigerator ...12
reindeer ...55
restaurant ...22
rhinoceros ...41
ribbons ...16
rice ...15
riding ...54
right ...61
river ...32
road ...23, 33
robot ...43
rocket ...31
rocks ...46
roller skates ...24
rolling pin ...12
roof ...9, 29
rooster ...37
roots ...35
rope ...21
rose ...18
rough ...60
rubber gloves ...12
ruler ...45
running ...53

Sad ...60
safety belt ...29
sail ...47
sailboat ...47
sailing ...51
salad ...14
sand ...46
sandals ...6
sandbox ...24
sandcastle ...46
sandpaper ...21
sandwich ...14
Santa Claus ...55
Saturday ...48
saucepan ...13
saucer ...13
saw ...21
sawdust ...21
scaffolding ...23
scales ...40
scarf ...7
scissors ...44
screwdriver ...21
screws ...21
sea ...46
seagulls ...47
seasons ...49
seaweed ...46
second ...59
sedan ...28
seed tray ...19
seedlings ...19
seeds ...19
seesaw ...25
September ...48
seven ...57
seventeen ...57
sewing ...43

sewing machine ...10
shampoo ...16
shapes ...56
shark ...40
shaving brush ...17
shaving cream ...17
sheep ...36
shelf ...20
shell ...38, 46
shoes ...6
shopping cart ...27
short ...61
shorts ...6
shoulder ...5
shouting ...53
shovel ...47
shower ...17
shut ...60
shutters ...8
sink ...13, 16
sister ...9
sitting ...53
six ...57
sixteen ...57
skateboard ...25
skating ...50
skiing ...50
skipping ...54
skirt ...7
skis ...50
skyscraper ...23
sleeping ...53
sleigh ...55
slide ...25
slip ...7
slippers ...6
slow ...60
smiling ...53
smooth ...60
snail ...19
snake ...41
sneakers ...6
snorkel ...51
snow ...49
snowman ...49
snowsuit ...7
soap ...17
soap frog ...17
soccer ...51
soccer ball ...51
socks ...6
soft ...60
soil ...18
soldiers ...42
spade ...19
spaghetti ...15
speedometer ...28
spinning top ...42
sponges ...16
spoon ...12
sports car ...28
spring ...49
square ...56
squirrel ...34
stable ...37
stadium ...23
staircase ...8
stalls ...22
standing ...53
star ...56
starfish ...46

station wagon ...29, 31
statue ...24
steering wheel ...28
stem ...18
stepladder ...21
steps ...9
stomach ...5
stool ...10
stove ...8, 12
strainer ...12
straw hat ...6
strawberries ...15
stream ...32
street lamp ...23
stroller ...24
submarine ...30
sugar ...14
summer ...49
sun ...49
sun hat ...47
Sunday ...48
sunflower ...18
sunglasses ...47
suppertime ...48
suspenders ...6
swan ...25
sweater ...6
sweatpants ...7
sweatshirt ...7
sweeping ...52
swimming pool ...22
swimsuit ...47
swing ...25
sword ...55

T-shirt ...6
table ...11
table-tennis paddle ...51
tacks ...21
tadpoles ...38
tail ...38
taking ...52
talcum powder ...16
talking ...53
tape measure ...20
tarts ...14
taxicab ...30
teacher ...45
teapot ...13
teddy bear ...42
teeth ...4
telephone ...10
telephone booth ...22
television ...11
ten ...57
tennis ...51
tennis racket ...51
tent ...33
theater ...22
thermometer ...11
thermos ...25
thin ...60
third ...59
thirteen ...57
thread ...43
three ...57
throwing ...54
thumb ...4
Thursday ...48
tidal pool ...47
tiger ...40

tights ...7
time ...48
tire ...28
tissues ...17
toad ...32
toadstools ...35
toast ...15
toe ...5
toilet ...17
toilet paper ...26
tomatoes ...14
tool box ...20
toothbrush ...16
toothpaste ...16
top ...59
towel ...16
toy car ...42
toy duck ...17
toy horse ...43
tractor ...36
traffic circle ...23
traffic lights ...23
trailer ...36
train ...31
train set ...42
train tracks ...30
tree ...34
triangle ...44, 56
tricycle ...24
trough ...36
trowel ...18
truck ...30
trunk ...29, 34, 41
Tuesday ...48
tulips ...19
turn indicator ...28
turntable ...10
turtle ...38
tusk ...41
twelve ...57
twenty ...57
twig ...35
twine ...18
two ...57

Umbrella ...7
under ...59
underpants ...6
undershirt ...6
up ...59

Vacuum cleaner ...10
valley ...32
vegetables ...27
village ...32
vintage car ...29
violin ...44

Walking ...53
wall ...9
wallpaper ...8
washcloth ...17
washing machine ...13
wasp ...18
watch ...6
water ...16
water wings ...47
waterfall ...33
watering can ...19
waterlilies ...32
waves ...46

weather ...49
Wednesday ...48
weeds ...19
week ...48
wet ...60
wheatfield ...36
wheel ...28
wheelbarrow ...19
whiskers ...38
whispering ...53
whistle ...42
white ...56
wildflowers ...33
window ...9
window box ...9
windowsill ...9
windshield ...29
windshield wipers ...29
windy ...49
wing ...39
winter ...49
wires ...21
witch ...55
wizard ...55
wood ...20
woodpecker ...35
wool hat ...6
workbench ...20
worms ...19
wrench ...21
wrist ...4
writing ...45

Year ...48
yellow ...56
yogurt ...15

Zebra ...41
zucchini ...27